PARENTS, OBEY YOUR CHILDREN

Volume I

PARENTS, OBEY YOUR CHILDREN

Volume I

CORETHA GANTLING
Affectionately known as Sister G

Cover image courtesy of https://creativecommons.org/licenses

Published by:

McDougal & Associates
www.thepublishedword.com

McDougal & Associates is an organization dedicated to the spreading the Gospel of the Lord Jesus Christ to as many people as possible in the shortest time possible.

ISBN: 978-1-964665-25-2

Printed on demand in the U.S., the U.K. and Australia
For Worldwide Distribution

Dedication

I dedicate this book to:

Father God, who gave parents instructions on training their children HIS WAY.

To my parents and my sister, who trained me in the
way I should go.

Acknowledgements

I acknowledge all the people God commissioned to teach me His WORD, especially my pastor, who encouraged me and started me on the path of teaching children in Sunday school when I was just 17 and my professors at Southwestern Christian College and Abilene Christian College. I thank God for you.

Contents

Introduction 9

1. Parents, Obey Your Children..........................11

2. Children, Train Your Parents.........................19

3. The Belt or the Bullet? 25

4. Avoiding Parental Provocation.....................35

5. Parents Are To Rule, Not Children..............39

6. Help Me, Lord! I Really Messed Up!...........43

7. Each of Us Will Answer To God 47

What God Has Said 51

Other Books by Coretha Gantling 65

Introduction

In our modern-day society, many of this generation don't know that Father God has given specific instructions on how to train our children. Proverbs 22:6 says clearly, *"Train up a child in the way he should go: and when he is old, he will not depart from it."* Thank God that He has set in place men and women who are experienced parents to teach the younger generations how to train their children in His ways.

The Word of God instructs older men (see Titus 2) to encourage and guide younger men toward wisdom, self-control, and good works, setting an example through their own lives and teaching others with integrity. Older women are instructed to teach younger women to love their husbands, to love their children, to be discreet, chaste, keepers at home, good, obedient to their own husbands, *"that the Word of God be not blasphemed."*

Our ignorance of God's ways in this regard has created a crisis situation in our country, a crisis in which our children are no longer subject to parents (or any other authority figure) and are, therefore, acting out instead of learning and developing as they should. Instead of being blessed by God, our children are frequenting juvenile reform centers and prisons and, sadly, are producing another lost generation they have no idea how to raise. Something has to be done to keep our little ones from a life of crime and debauchery, to keep them from a premature death.

In response to this current crisis of parenthood, God has given me this little book. It gives simple but effective teachings about how we can rescue our children from chaos and destruction. The answer is to train our sons and daughters God's way.

Coretha Gantling,
Jacksonville, Florida

Chapter 1

Parents, Obey Your Children in the Lord

**Parents, obey your
children in the Lord:
for this is right.**
— 1ˢᵀ Children's 6:1

Yes, I know what the Bible says:

*Children, obey your parents in the Lord: for this
is right. Honour thy father and mother; which
is the first commandment with promise; that
it may be well with thee, and thou mayest live
long on the earth.* Ephesians 6:1-3

Parents, Obey Your Children

I know what Proverbs 22:6 says:

> *Train up a child in the way he should go: and when he is old, he will not depart from it.*

I know, but, as I'm sure you are aware, since you are living in the twenty-first century, things have changed dramatically for this generation. A child living today may not have a Bible, and it's even possible he or she has never seen one. Because of this, they may not know or care what the Bible says. To them, the Bible may be just another ordinary book. They have no idea that the Word of God has great power, nor do they know what the Bible actually says. Therefore, it's no wonder they don't seem to care what God has to say to them in His written or spoken Word. Instead, their own words are considered top priority. Why is this? Children today have been taught that their words control their destiny.

Many parents gave birth to these children at a young age and were not ready to train even a puppy dog, let alone a child, a living, breathing human being. The mothers are little more than young girls who only recently stopped playing with baby dolls, and they are, therefore, in no way prepared to trade a baby doll for a real live baby.

A child living today may not have

a Bible, and it's even possible he or

she has never seen one. Because of

this, they may not know or care what

the Bible says!

When these children, now parents themselves, were conceived, their mamas and daddies were dealing with "the teen scene," their hormones were raging, and they were unchecked and fancy free. In 1966 James Brown wrote the song "It's a Man's Man's Man's World." Since then, things have changed. Today the real tune is: "This Is a Child's World." In far too many families, children rule their parents.

Parental supervision and guidance have become a thing of the past. Now children do their own thing. They make their own rules, as well as create and lay down rules for their parents. They boldly tell their parents what to do and what not to do. They let their parents know what they want to eat and what they will not eat. They even decide who will sleep in their room. For the most part, the rules they create are for their parents, not for themselves. They decide who comes and goes in the house where they live, even though they don't pay the house note or rent. In this way, many of today's children have turned their rooms into mini motels.

Even though today's children never share in the financial obligations of the household, their rooms are somehow off limits to their parents. What is done there is no business of anyone else, they believe.

They go where they want to go and come as they please without any curfews. No wonder the babies they now have in place of their dolls are also treated like dolls. Diapers are changed or not changed. Babies are fed on an instant milk formula of some kind, as breast milk has become a thing of the past for this generation. The breasts of our young girls now serve as cover for their cell phones.

Today's young mothers tune into Facebook for child rearing suggestions or rely on their friends' advice. "Mother's wit" is a thing of the past. Now young daughters tell their mothers what they will or will not wear, and many choose to wear clothes that make them look like they were poured into them, clothes that are so tight they show all their private parts from top to bottom.

Today a father may or may not be present in the home or even in the lives of his children. Many young boys openly share with their dad what their girlfriends allow them to do to their bodies, as if their dad were just another friend, not the man who gave them birth and is responsible for their upbringing.

Today sons and daughters text their parents what they want them to bring home for dinner. Nutritious meals have become a thing of the past. What appeals to a child's taste buds has replaced foods that will keep them healthy and well. No wonder childhood diseases and the effects of malnutrition are rampant today!

Fast foods, which have little or no nutrients for the brain, let alone for the rest of the body, have replaced the nutritious meals of bygone eras. Brain foods, which are essential to the development and sustenance of the human brain and can keep the entire body healthy, are sorely missing from family diets today. We have become a grab-and-go generation. Fast food of all kinds has replaced essential elements that can keep this generation healthy and alert so they can focus and learn and develop properly.

Tragically, many minors are already raising their own children, without having any knowledge, understanding, or experience about child rearing. This is very sad! Often they refuse to listen to their mother or grandmother, women who do have knowledge, understanding, and experience on this subject. These older generations, more importantly, have knowledge about training a child in God's way.

What appeals to a child's taste buds has replaced foods that will keep them healthy and well. No wonder childhood diseases and the effects of malnutrition are rampant today!

Mothers of past generations had a gift we called "Mother Wit." What is Mother Wit? It is a gift from God, a discernment concerning the do's and don'ts of child rearing. Much of this Mother Wit came from a knowledge of God's Word. Titus 2, for example, instructs older men to live lives of example before younger men and older women to instruct younger women how to love their husbands and care for their children. Today, frustration and upset are constantly arising because our young mothers are not taught how to handle day-to-day situations with a tiny baby who needs their constant attention.

Whose fault is all of this? God laid the responsibility squarely on the parents when He commanded:

> *Train up a child in the way he should go: and when he is old, he will not depart from it.*
>
> Proverbs 22:6

Clearly, we are now suffering the results of our disobedience to God's Word.

Chapter 2

Children, Train Your Parents

Train up your parents in the way they should go: and when they are old, they will not depart from it.
2ND Childhood 22:6

Training parents is not an easy job. It requires skill, knowledge, and focus, as well as observation. Children become very good at training parents once they acquire skill and knowledge through observation and focus. Because children do not have to go to work daily or have the responsibility of paying bills etc., this allows them time to observe their parents and to learn to manipulate them to follow their instructions.

Very early in life, children learn how to control and manipulate their parents, even from the crib. Children watch, listen to, and observe their parents' daily habits. They are smart enough to know when strategy #1 isn't working, and they move to strategy #2. And they keep changing tactics until they find a strategy that works. They are very consistent and persistent.

Yes, children begin training their parents from the crib. They cry, scream, and kick until they are allowed to do what they want. This is control by negative behavior. As the children grow from infancy to tots and from children to teenagers, this behavior is perfected and worsens. These days parents can't even bribe their children to behave well.

If this type of negative behavior is not redirected at an early age—usually before the child reaches the age of four or five—the negative behavior will then escalate. And, once a child has taken control of his or her parents, it is very difficult to reverse the situation, and parents find themselves in a very serious dilemma.

Children who have too much idle time become forceful, belligerent, and determined to have their own way—at home, at school, and anywhere else. To break this vicious cycle, parents resort to attending parenting classes in an attempt to learn

Children begin training their parents from the crib. They cry, scream, and kick until they are allowed to do what they want. This is control by negative behavior!

how to get control of their situation. It would be so much better for parents to train their children from the beginning in God's way. If children are not taught God's way, the devil will teach them his way. It's a simple as that.

Contrary to popular belief, the belt (the rod of correction) that God has placed in our hands, as parents, can resolve negative behaviors, and therefore must be used when necessary. Many now consider this to be child abuse, but God gave specific instructions to parents, and He did it because He loves children and wants to protect them from the consequences of bad behavior. It's time to stop ignoring God's instructions and recognize that He always knows best.

The now popularized method of child discipline, the "time-out," cannot be found anywhere in God's Word. Although the once popular phrase, "Spare the rod and spoil the child," also is not found in the Bible, God does have much to say about this important subject. For instance:

> *Whoever spares the rod hates their children,*
> *but the one who loves their children is careful*
> *to discipline them.*   Proverbs 13:24, NIV

Contrary to popular belief, the belt (the rod of correction) that God has placed in our hands, as parents, can resolve negative behaviors, and therefore must be used when necessary. Many now consider this to be child abuse, but God gave specific instructions to parents, and He did it because He loves children and wants to protect them from the consequences of bad behavior!

God Almighty knew before your child was born what would work and what would not. We parents need to ask God to teach us and help us as we raise and train our children, and we need to do things His way.

I'm sure you have noticed that since discipline has been neglected in both the home and the school, our children are being murdered at an alarming rate. These are precious souls that have been entrusted to our care, so we are responsible to do something about this tragic loss.

Chapter 3

The Belt or the Bullet?

*Folly is bound up in the heart of a child,
but the rod of discipline will drive it far
away.* Proverbs 22:15, NIV

Ever since proper discipline has been banned from our nation's schools, our children have been exposed to the bullet. The belt is a rod of correction, but the bullet is a rod of destruction.

In many of our schools, very little learning is now taking place. Sadly, our children lack the wisdom to understand the importance of getting an education. So, what do they do? They carry on with foolishness in our classrooms. God said that foolishness (or folly) is *"bound up in the heart of a child."* What's the remedy? He said it was *"the rod of discipline."*

Our children are disrespectful to their teachers, who are there to educate, train, and protect them! This happens because the children have first been allowed to disrespect their parents, those who gave them life, those who provide for their daily needs, and are responsible for their success in life. Modern children not only disrespect parents and teachers; they disrespect anyone and everyone who has been put in place to help them, protect them, and train them. This is dangerous!

Because the bullet has now replaced the rod of correction, we must have security guards or policemen stationed at the entrance of our schools. They come with their belt of bullets, hoping to protect our children, but they's still dying at alarming numbers. Who will die next in our schools—this year, next year, or in the future? As parents, we are called to provide for, protect, teach, and train our children. When we fail at that task, this is the kind of tragedy that ensues. Many children now live in constant fear and are asking the question: "Will I be the next one to die?"

Yes, in the twenty-first century, our children live in fear every day. They leave home, going

Modern children not only disrespect parents and teachers; they disrespect anyone and everyone who has been put in place to help them, protect them, and train them. This is dangerous!

to school, to the park, or to the store, not know-
ing if they will return home safely or not. We
are now forced to train our children to pay attention to their surroundings, to put their cell
phones away and keep watch for suspicious
people or vehicles approaching them. Every
parent now has to take the time to have this
discussion with their children, and we have to
listen to them as well.

If we had only listened to God and obeyed
His instructions, this life on the edge could
have been avoided. God had called us to teach
our children:

1. To love God, themselves, and others.
2. To listen to and follow instructions the first
   time they are given.
3. To choose to do the right thing and reject
   the wrong.
4. To know and understand that school is a
   place to gain academic knowledge that will
   help prepare them for a successful future.
5. To respect their parents and all those
   who are in authority—in the home, in
   the church, in the school, and in the
   community.

God had called us to teach our children:

1. **To love God, themselves, and others.**
2. **To listen to and follow instructions the first time they are given.**
3. **To choose to do the right thing and reject the wrong.**
4. **To know and understand that school is a place to gain academic knowledge that will help prepare them for a successful future.**
5. **To respect their parents and all those who are in authority—in the home, in the church, in the school, and in the community.**

Have you ever noticed that after you use the rod of correction, your child's negative behavior changes? Have you noticed that when your child needs the rod again, they will usually misbehave until the rod is used? God, who created them, knew this and taught us:

> *Discipline your children, and they will give you peace;*
> > *they will bring you the delights you desire.*
> > > Proverbs 29:17, NIV

Proverbs 23:14 even shows us that proper discipline will save your child from death:

> *Do not withhold discipline from a child;*
> > *if you punish them with the rod, they will not die.* (NIV)

Today, in the twenty-first century, American children are all too often raising and training themselves. Many of them are in single-parent homes where the only parent is distracted by, infatuated with, and addicted to social media on their cell phones or iPad. Many of these parents have not accepted their children as a blessing from God, resent their intrusion into their social life, and refuse to give them the loving care they need in order to form stable lives.

Sadly, these parents can even be heard "cussing out" their babies in language that is foul, offensive, and obscene. These are words you don't even want your dog to hear, and they cut to the heart of any child. This is just the opposite of the loving care God demands of us as parents.

Have we traded our children for a puppy or a dog? We spend lots of time with our puppies, training them to obey so that when they get older, they will not be difficult to manage. Do you believe what God said in Proverbs 22:6, that if we train up a child in the way he or she should go, when they are old, they will not depart from it? Have you read anywhere in the Bible about training your dog? How much time do we really spend training our children in God's ways?

We spend our precious time and hard-earned money to take our pets to obedience school. Why? So that they will learn to follow our instructions and do it the first time those instructions are given. But how many times do we repeat the same thing to our children, and they don't seem to hear or respond?

We give our pets rewards for obeying and consequences for disobeying. Wouldn't life be easier if we trained our children to follow instructions in this same way?

We inquire about and purchase top quality food for our dogs, but we ask our children what they want to eat instead of training them to eat nutritiously so that they can stay healthy.

Even when we're tired, if our dog wants to play ball, we manage to summon up the energy to comply. To the children that we birthed, we say, "Honey I am so tired. I worked hard all day." And we overlook the sadness on their faces when we say no to their pleas for attention.

We need to cry out to God for forgiveness and seek His help to be a better parent:

Lord, forgive us for not spending quality time with our children, for we know not when You may call us or them to leave this earth and meet You face to face. Forgive us when we are on our cell phones instead of praying for and guiding our children. Forgive us for being on Facebook instead of being in the faces of the children You placed in our care. Help us to teach them that You are the only God and to do it from the time they get up until they go to bed

We give our pets rewards for obeying and consequences for disobeying. Wouldn't life be easier if we trained our children to follow instructions in this same way?

Parents, Obey Your Children

at night (see Deuteronomy 6). Help us to teach them that You want them to come to You and be part of Your eternal Kingdom (see Matthew 19:14).

Amen!

Chapter 4

Avoiding Parental Provocation

Fathers, do not embitter your children, or they will become discouraged.

Colossians 3:21, NIV

Parental provocation can cause vicious anger in a child. Children are human, and they get angry, just as adults do. When a father or mother constantly criticizes or belittles a child over a period of time, that child can become wounded and angry, even to the point of becoming vicious. A deep wound that is constantly intruded upon can cause irritation, annoyance, and eventually, rage.

Most parents fail to realize when they are provoking their child. Sometimes parents unknowingly take their frustrations and anger out on their children, verbally abusing them and sometimes striking them. They are trying to release their own tensions and frustrations, but they are doing it at the expense of their precious child.

It's very discouraging to a child when a parent constantly provokes them. It's difficult to obey and honor a parent who embitters you. Parents need to redirect their anger by having an outlet—like playing ball, jogging, going out with friends, taking family outings, etc.

Instead of belittling our children, as parents, we must find ways to encourage them. We should encourage them with words and also with loving actions. This will help build their self-esteem.

We must teach our children through our example as well as through our words. When we discover ways to encourage them, we will notice them beginning to develop a positive self-image. And developing a positive self-imagine is key to bringing out the greatness God put on the inside of them. Then, they will begin to experience success in all areas of their lives, as God intended.

It's very discouraging to a child

when a parent constantly provokes

them. It's difficult to obey and honor

a parent who embitters you. Parents

need to redirect their anger!

Chapter 5

Parents Are To Rule, Not Children

> *A rod and a reprimand impart wisdom,*
> *but a child left undisciplined disgraces its*
> *mother.*   Proverbs 29:15, NIV

When parents rule, households are more peaceful and unified. Parents who take charge of their households have effective rules and guidelines, and they teach these rules and guidelines to their children and then enforce them as needed. When parents take charge of their children in this way, the children become emotionally stable and agreeable. This is God's way.

Yes, God has a plan for parents that works in training and teaching children. When parents follow God's plan for their children, the tug of war, most especially during the early years of their children's lives, ends. From birth to about five years of age are very crucial years for children to learn obedience and receive training and discipline from their parents.

Under the best circumstances, parenting is difficult. This difficulty is multiplied many times over when parents neglect to follow God's laws for training their children. God said:

> *Foolishness is bound in the heart of a child; but the rod of correction shall drive it far from him.*
>
> Proverbs 22:15

Most modern parents are very permissive. They allow their children to do whatever they want to do. The children get to decide what to eat, what to wear, where to go, etc. But children have no prior experience making choices that will affect their daily lives and their future. Later, when they begin to rebel and become so obstinate that the parents have no control over them, the parents finally realize their mistake.

When children become defiant and overrule whatever their parent say, this is too often the

Under the best circumstances, parenting is difficult. This difficulty is multiplied many times over when parents neglect to follow God's laws for training their children!

point when the parents begin to seek help. They now realize the need to regain control and regain their children's respect and honor. However, parents soon learn that it will take an act of God to change this seemingly-hopeless situation. When we neglect to teach our children when they are very young about God, Jesus, and the Holy Spirit, we inadvertently teach them about the devil and his ways.

When we teach our children the principles of God at a young age, we are protecting them and preparing them for a life of hope, a life that is rooted and grounded in love for God and all mankind. It is sad that parents often wait to seek help until their children become defiant and stop respecting their authority. This may well be too late to regain control and earn the respect and compliance of their children. The results can be seen in our nation's prisons.

Chapter 6

Help Me, Lord! I Really Messed Up!

Call unto me, and I will answer thee, and show thee great and mighty things, which thou knowest not.   Jeremiah 33:3

God is always ready to help us when we're ready to seek His help. But don't wait until it's too late. Cry out to God today.

Lord, help me to consult You on how to straighten out the mess I made when I neglected my parental duties. I realize now that things are out control in our household, and I need You to intervene. As the song says, "Lord, if you don't do it, it won't get done." Lord, fix it for our household. We have a problem that only

You can solve. So, Lord do it for us. Thank You, Lord, for fixing this situation.

You warned us as parents, but we did not listen. We refused to obey Your plan for training up our children Your way. Now that things are out of control, we desperately need Your help. Lord, teach us how to train our children Your way.

Many parents today are not as responsible for their children's well-being as parents from generations past. God specifically assigned to parents the responsibility of taking care of the total child — the physical, mental, emotional, and spiritual well-being of each one He birthed through them. But, sadly, today's parents seem too busy and/or preoccupied with their own desires and well-being to think about their child's welfare.

Modern technology has provided digital baby-sitters for infants, toddlers, and all the way up to teens. The cellphone, the iPad, and the computer have replaced human hands that should hold, rock, and cuddle children. Whether in Walmart, at home, in restaurants, or in church, we see babies with a gadget of some kind in front of them. These gadgets have

God specifically assigned to parents the responsibility of taking care of the total child—the physical, mental, emotional, and spiritual well-being of each one He birthed through them. But, sadly, today's parents seem too busy and/or preoccupied with their own desires and well-being to think about their child's welfare!

become addictive f\or the youngest to the oldest child.

The dads and moms have their own set of gadgets as well, and these distract them from their vital childcare duties. These are duties like feeding, changing diapers, bathing their children, and other necessary responsibilities.

In all of this, what unspoken messages are we giving our children? Are we conveying messages of acceptance or rejection? Approval or disapproval? Care or indifference? As parents, we must nurture each of our children daily, not just when we feel like it. We must provide love, protection, and the necessities of life. Deuteronomy 6 shows us that parents must daily instruct and train their children. Are we doing that?

Chapter 7

Each of Us Will Answer to God

In those days they shall say no more, The fathers have eaten sour grapes, and the children's teeth are set on edge. Jeremiah 31:29, ASV

God is so good, kind, and merciful that our children no longer need to suffer for the mistakes we made in the past. His Word tells us we are only accountable for our own sins, not the sins of another, including those of our parents.

> *The soul who sins shall die. The son shall not bear the guilt of the father, nor the father bear the guilt of the son. The righteousness of the righteous shall be upon himself, and the wickedness of the wicked shall be upon himself.*
> Ezekiel 18:20, NKJV

Parents, Obey Your Children

According to the Bible, we must each ask God to forgive us for our own sins, not the sins of our parents, nor of the generations before them. In Old Testament times, there were cases in which children suffered because their parents sinned. David and Bathsheba's first-born son died (see 2 Samuel 12). Lot's children became more worldly than he was (see Genesis 19). In general, the sins of the Israelite people affected their children as well as themselves. With the coming of Jesus and the dawn of the New Testament, that all changed. Thank God for His grace and mercy extended to us today. We can find redemption through Christ, and, as parents, we can chart a better way forward for ourselves and our children.

According to the Bible, we must each ask God to forgive us for our own sins, not the sins of our parents, nor of the generations before them!

What God Has Said

In everything we do in life, including parenting, we would be wise to always pay attention to and follow what God says. After all, He is the One who created us, so He knows best in every circumstance. Here are some things God has said concerning this subject of parenting. The following scriptural passages are ALL from the New Living Translation of the Bible.

ABOUT A PARENT'S RESPONSIBILITY
TO DISCIPLINE THEIR CHILDREN

Those who spare the rod of discipline hate their children.
Those who love their children care enough to discipline them.   Proverbs 13:24

Parents, Obey Your Children

Discipline your children while there is hope.
Otherwise you will ruin their lives.

Proverbs 19:18

A youngster's heart is filled with foolishness,
but physical discipline will drive it far
away. Proverbs 22:15

Don't fail to discipline your children.
The rod of punishment won't kill them.
Physical discipline
may well save them from death.

Proverbs 23:13-14

To discipline a child produces wisdom,
but a mother is disgraced by an undisciplined
child.
When the wicked are in authority, sin flourishes,
but the godly will live to see their downfall.
Discipline your children, and they will give you
peace of mind
and will make your heart glad.

Proverbs 29:15-17

THAT CORRECTION AND DISCIPLINE ARE A NORMAN AND HEALTHY PART OF OUR PARENTAL RESPONSIBILITY

Since we respected our earthly fathers who disciplined us, shouldn't we submit even more to the discipline of the Father of our spirits, and live forever?　　　　Hebrews 12:9

And you know that we treated each of you as a father treats his own children.
　　　　1 Thessalonians 2:11

To learn, you must love discipline;
　　it is stupid to hate correction.
　　　　　　Proverbs 12:1

Think about it: Just as a parent disciplines a child, the LORD your God disciplines you for your own good.　　　　Deuteronomy 8:5

Yet when we are judged by the Lord, we are being disciplined so that we will not be condemned along with the world.　　1 Corinthians 11:32

I correct and discipline everyone I love. So be diligent and turn from your indifference.

Revelation 3:19

But consider the joy of those corrected by God!
  Do not despise the discipline of the Almighty
  when you sin.   *Job 5:17*

My child, don't reject the LORD's discipline,
  and don't be upset when he corrects you.
For the LORD corrects those he loves,
  just as a father corrects a child in whom he
  delights.   Proverbs 3:11-12

GOD HAS PROMISED TO BLESS OBEDIENT AND RESPECTFUL CHILDREN

Honor your father and mother. Then you will live a long, full life in the land the LORD your God is giving you.   Exodus 20:12

Each of you must show great respect for your mother and father, and you must always observe my Sabbath days of rest. I am the LORD your God.   Leviticus 19:3

Children, always obey your parents, for this pleases the LORD.   Colossians 3:20

Children, obey your parents because you belong to the Lord, for this is the right thing to do. "Honor your father and mother." This is the first commandment with a promise: If you honor your father and mother, "things will go well for you, and you will have a long life on the earth."   Ephesians 6:1-3

SOLOMON, OFTEN CALLED THE WISEST MAN WHO EVER LIVED, SPENT MUCH OF HIS PROVERBS TEACHING CHILDREN TO RESPECT AND OBEY THEIR PARENTS

My child, listen when your father corrects you.
Don't neglect your mother's instruction.
What you learn from them will crown you with grace
and be a chain of honor around your neck.
                    Proverbs 1:8-9

Parents, Obey Your Children

My child, never forget the things I have taught
   you.
   Store my commands in your heart.
If you do this, you will live many years,
   and your life will be satisfying.
Never let loyalty and kindness leave you!
   Tie them around your neck as a reminder.
   Write them deep within your heart.
Then you will find favor with both God and
   people,
   and you will earn a good reputation.

Proverbs 3:1-4

My son, obey your father's commands,
   and don't neglect your mother's instruction.
Keep their words always in your heart.
   Tie them around your neck.
When you walk, their counsel will lead you.
   When you sleep, they will protect you.
   When you wake up, they will advise you.
For their command is a lamp
   and their instruction a light;
   their corrective discipline
   is the way to life.   Proverbs 6:20-23

Follow my advice, my son;
   always treasure my commands.
Obey my commands and live!
   Guard my instructions as you guard your
   own eyes.
Tie them on your fingers as a reminder.
   Write them deep within your heart.
Love wisdom like a sister;
   make insight a beloved member of your family.
                                    Proverbs 7:1-4

A wise child accepts a parent's discipline;
   a mocker refuses to listen to correction.
                                    Proverbs 13:1

Listen to your father, who gave you life,
   and don't despise your mother when she is
   old.   Proverbs 23:22

The eye that mocks a father
   and despises a mother's instructions
will be plucked out by ravens of the valley
   and eaten by vultures.   Proverbs 30:17

DAVID BECAME A GREAT KING BECAUSE HE LEARNED OBEDIENCE TO HIS PARENTS AND RESPECT FOR AUTHORITY

So David left the sheep with another shepherd and set out early the next morning with the gifts, AS JESSE HAD DIRECTED HIM. He arrived at the camp just as the Israelite army was leaving for the battlefield with shouts and battle cries.

1 Samuel 17:20, Emphasis Mine

ESTHER BECAME QUEEN BECAUSE SHE HAD LEARNED TO RESPECT AND OBEY THE UNCLE WHO RAISED HER

Esther continued to keep her family background and nationality a secret. SHE WAS STILL FOLLOWING MORDECAI'S DIREC-TIONS, just as she did when she lived in his home.   Esther 2:20, Emphasis Mine

JACOB WAS BLESSED BECAUSE OF HIS OBEDIENCE TO HIS PARENTS

He also knew that JACOB HAD OBEYED HIS PARENTS and gone to Paddan-aram.
Genesis 28:7, Emphasis Mine

JOSEPH, EVEN AFTER BECOMING THE PRIME MINISTER OF EGYPT, CONTINUED TO SHOW RESPECT TO HIS FATHER

"Now hurry back to my father and tell him, 'This is what your son Joseph says: God has made me master over all the land of Egypt. So come down to me immediately! You can live in the region of Goshen, where you can be near me with all your children and grandchildren, your flocks and herds, and everything you own. I will take care of you there, for there are still five years of famine ahead of us. Otherwise you, your household, and all your animals will starve.'"
Genesis 45:9-11

Joseph prepared his chariot and traveled to Goshen to meet his father, Jacob. When Joseph

arrived, he embraced his father and wept, hold-
ing him for a long time.   Genesis 46:29

So Joseph assigned the best land of Egypt—the
region of Rameses—to his father and his brothers, and he settled them there, just as Pharaoh
had commanded. And Joseph provided food for
his father and his brothers in amounts appropri-
ate to the number of their dependents, including
the smallest children.   Genesis 47:11-12

JESUS IS OUR GREATEST EXAMPLE IN ALL THINGS. AS LONG AS HE WALKED IN FLESH ON THIS EARTH, HE WAS OBEDIENT TO HIS EARTHLY PARENTS

Then he returned to Nazareth with them and
<u>was obedient to them</u>. And his mother stored all
these things in her heart.   Luke 2:51

Even though Jesus was God's Son, <u>he learned
obedience</u> from the things he suffered.
                                        Hebrews 5:8

GOD COMMENDS PARENTS WHO
DISCIPLINE THEIR CHILDREN

I have singled him [Abraham] out so that he will direct his sons and their families to keep the way of the LORD by doing what is right and just. Then I will do for Abraham all that I have promised.   Genesis 18:19

WISE AND FIRM PARENTING WAS A FACTOR
CONSIDERED BY THE EARLY CHURCH
WHEN CHOOSING THEIR LEADERS

He must manage his own family well, having children who respect and obey him.
                              1 Timothy 3:4

A deacon must be faithful to his wife, and he must manage his children and household well.
                              1 Timothy 3:12

An elder must live a blameless life. He must be faithful to his wife, and his children must be believers who don't have a reputation for being wild or rebellious.   Titus 1:6

Parents, Obey Your Children

THROUGH SOLOMON, GOD PROMISED THAT WE WOULD NEVER REGRET EXERCISING PROPER DISCIPLINE WITH OUR CHILDREN

A wise child brings joy to a father;
a foolish child brings grief to a mother.

Proverbs 10:1

WHAT GOD SAID TO TITUS

As for you, Titus, promote the kind of living that reflects wholesome teaching. Teach the older men to exercise self-control, to be worthy of respect, and to live wisely. They must have sound faith and be filled with love and patience. Similarly, teach the older women to live in a way that honors God. They must not slander others or be heavy drinkers. Instead, they should teach others what is good. These older women must train the younger women to love their husbands and their children, to live wisely and be pure, to work in their homes, to do good, and to be submissive to their husbands. Then they will not bring shame on the word of God.

Titus 2:1-5

WHAT GOD SAID TO ISRAEL THROUGH MOSES

You and your children and grandchildren must fear the LORD your God as long as you live. If you obey all his decrees and commands, you will enjoy a long life. Listen closely, Israel, and be careful to obey. Then all will go well with you, and you will have many children in the land flowing with milk and honey, just as the Lord, the God of your ancestors, promised you.

Deuteronomy 6:2-3

Now, it's your turn. Will you believe God or modern philosophies? The choice is yours today.

Other Books by Coretha Gantling

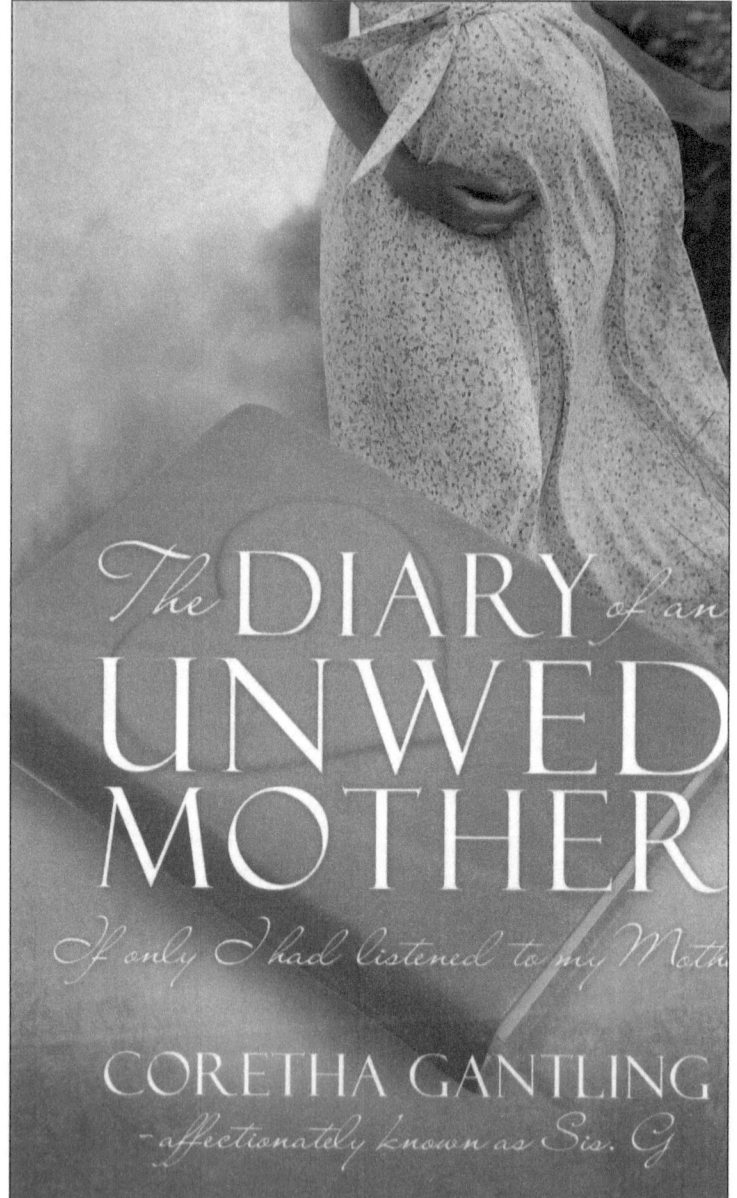

The DIARY of an
UNWED
MOTHER

If only I had listened to my Mother

CORETHA GANTLING
-affectionately known as Sis. G

The DIARY of an
UNWED
MOTHER
Volume 2
A New Beginning

CORETHA GANTLING
~affectionately known as Sis. G

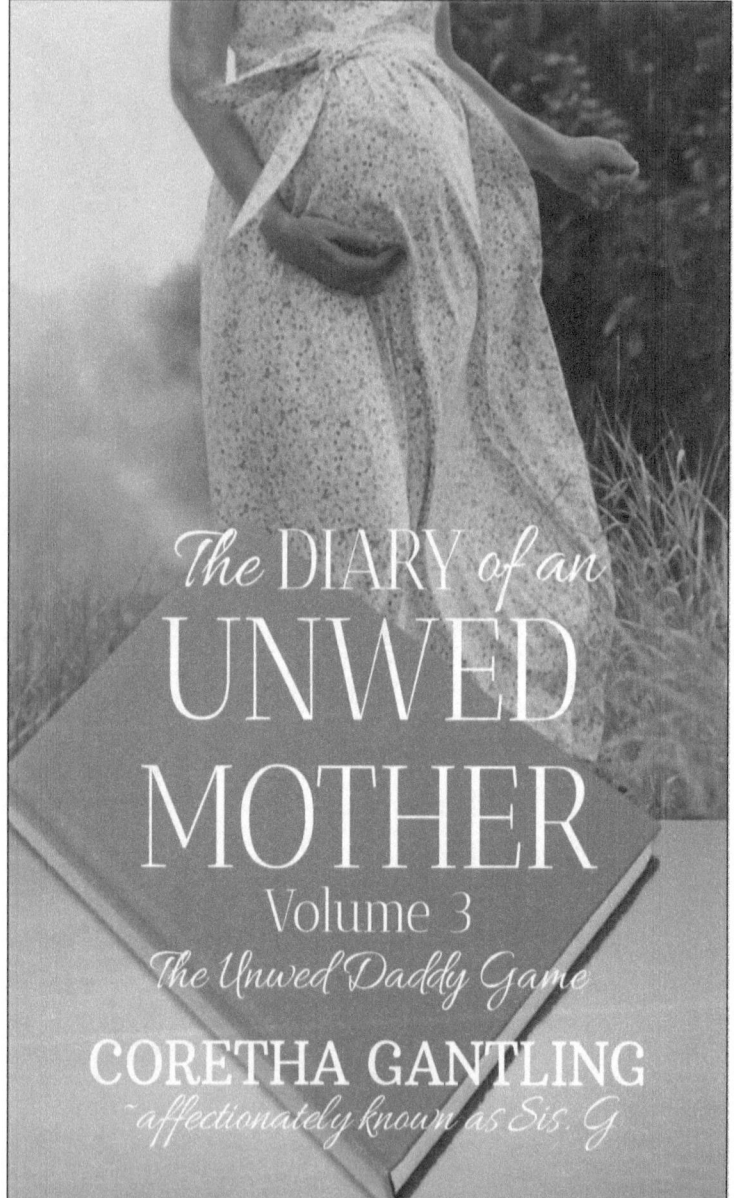

The DIARY *of an*
UNWED
MOTHER
Volume 3
The Unwed Daddy Game

CORETHA GANTLING
~affectionately known as Sis. G

The DIARY of an
UNWED
MOTHER

Volume 4
UNPLANNED AND UNWANTED
BUT SENT BY GOD

CORETHA GANTLING
~affectionately known as Sis. G

ALL MY ANIMAL FRIENDS COME TO CHURCH WITH ME

(11) Lenord Leopard
(12) Zinard Zebra
(10) Robinette Rabbit
(9) Horiska Horse
(8) Lenta Lion
① Patrick Panda
② Paulus Parrot
③ Katie Kangaroo
④ Lady Llama
⑤ Squarelena Squarrel
⑥ Mondrell Monkey
⑦ Ellie Mae Elephant

Story by Coretha Gautling
Illustrations by Coretha and Friends

JONATHAN AND HIS BIRTHDAY SURPRISES

Story by Coretha Gantling
Illustrations by Coretha and Friends

RUTHIE AND JOE GIVE THEIR LIVES TO JESUS

Story by Coretha Gautling
Illustrations by Coretha, Ruthie, and Joe

JOHN HENRY JOHNSON'S FIRST PEN PAL

Story and Illustrations by Coretha Gantling

 Coretha Gantling, affectionately known as Sister G, has loved children since she was a child herself. She began teaching Sunday school when she was just a teenager. Ms. Gantling graduated from Southwestern Christian College and Abilene Christian University and then taught children in 1st through 8th grades in public schools for twenty-nine years, using creative, effective teaching strategies and methods to help them search for and accomplish their purpose-driven life. She believes that with the right approach children from all walks of life, whether in public or private school or Sunday school, can have great success and become accomplished citizens in their communities and beyond.

Ms. Gantling believes that our children are our greatest asset and the key to our nation becoming more unified under God. She mentors young ladies, twelve to twenty-five, who are known as The Holy Ghost Girls. She teaches them how to sew and cook healthy and nutritious meals and otherwise trains them in God's way through life lessons from the Word of God. Currently she hosts a Tuesday Prayerline, interceding for the children of the world. She also teaches Wednesday Midweek Bible Study to senior citizens, Bible Storyland Radio Program on Saturday mornings. On Thursday evenings Sister G teaches University of Biblical Studies/Boyz 2 Men & Girlz 2 Ladyz.